TJ AND THE
SLEEPOVER

WRITTEN BY
Aviaq Johnston

ILLUSTRATED BY
Jesus Lopez

Table of Contents

CHAPTER 1
A Zombie Apocalypse!

I t was the beginning of spring, and the snow was melting fast. TJ woke up on a Saturday morning to the bright sun shining through his curtains. Spring was one of TJ's favourite times of the year. He went to the window and thought about what the day might bring.

The sky was bright blue, and the sun was rising high. There was no wind, and TJ could hear the early-morning songs of the snow buntings. *Wow!* TJ thought. *It feels like it's gonna be a good day!*

He got dressed and ran to the kitchen, where his *anaana* was drinking coffee. He got himself a bowl of cereal and started to eat quickly.

"Whoa, *irniq*," his anaana said. "What's the rush?"

TJ tried to smile without spilling milk from his mouth, but it still dripped down his chin. He answered, "It's so nice out! I want to go play out with my friends."

"Okay," said his anaana. "But make sure you dress warmly. Just because it looks nice out doesn't mean it's not cold."

"Yup!" TJ said just as he was about to slurp up the rest of the milk.

He got up from the table and went to brush his teeth. Then he got his outdoor clothes on and made his way over to his friend Sapa's house. TJ walked in without knocking and was greeted by Sapa's parents.

"Good morning, TJ!" said Sapa's anaana. "You're up bright and early."

"Good morning," TJ replied. "Is Sapa awake?"

"Yup!!" Sapa yelled as she came around a hallway corner. "Let's go play out?"

In a matter of moments, the two were outside and heading to the playground. They avoided the roads and walked through shortcuts between houses. Some places had dogs outside, but TJ and Sapa knew that the ropes tying them up weren't long enough to reach the well-worn path people had made during the winter.

When they got to the playground, there were only a few other kids already there. TJ and Sapa looked around and saw that the roads were lined with other children making their way to the playground.

"Check it out." TJ pointed to the children running toward the playground. "It looks like a zombie apocalypse!!!"

This began a huge game of zombie tag with the kids at the playground and the other kids arriving. The "zombies" couldn't go onto the playground equipment, but if they touched someone, that person became a zombie and had to try to tag the rest of the "humans."

After the game started, TJ saw his friends Martha, Robert, and Itani coming to join in.

"I'm gonna get you!" Itani yelled to TJ. Itani kept trying to tag TJ and turn him into a zombie. Every time TJ ducked into a new part of the play structure, Itani would follow him. Finally, Itani tagged TJ on the shoulder.

"Got you, got you, ha ha ha ha," Itani teased, pointing his finger at TJ and getting up close to his face. TJ found the teasing kind of annoying, but soon he got back into the game.

TJ was glad all his friends had come to the playground. He knew they were going to have a fun day!

CHAPTER 2
Playing Out

TJ and his friends spent the whole morning playing at the playground and around town. They played another round of zombie tag, then moved on to wolf tag, Red Rover, hide-and-seek, and *anauligaaq*.

TJ sure was having fun, but he couldn't help feeling like Itani was bothering him more than the others. During each game of tag they played, Itani was going straight for TJ and not any of the other kids. Even when they were playing hide-and-seek, Itani would follow him and try to be in the same hiding spots. TJ started to feel like he wanted some time away from Itani.

TJ thought about asking Itani to stop,

but he was worried that would make Itani mad, and then he'd bug TJ even more! He decided not to say anything. Everyone else seemed to be having a good time, so TJ thought maybe he was just overreacting.

After TJ's team won the game of anauligaaq, which took half the morning, Robert said, "Ugh, I'm so hungry!"

Itani said, "Me too! Let's go eat at my house. My stepmom said she was going to make bannock for us."

All together, TJ, Sapa, Martha, and Robert dreamily said, "Mmmmmm!"

They made their way to Itani's house, which was close to the playground. As they were about to go inside, Itani's *ataata* was coming out of the porch carrying a big white thing in his arms. "What's that, Ataata?" asked Itani.

"Hey, kids," said Itani's ataata. He turned to Itani. "This is your grandparents' tent! I was thinking I could put it up behind our house. Maybe you and your friends want to have a sleepover in it tonight?"

Itani loudly said, "Yeah!"

Then his ataata said, "Of course, as long as their parents are okay with it."

Itani said to his friends, "Let's eat fast, then go ask your parents, okay?"

The kids all agreed. TJ was trying to

be excited because he really enjoyed camping, but he wasn't looking forward to spending the night with Itani when he'd been bothering TJ all morning.

They entered the house to the wonderful smell of bannock. For a moment, TJ forgot all about his bad feelings. He thought about cartoons with characters following smells with their noses and silly expressions on their faces. TJ was sure that he and his friends looked like that as they went into the kitchen.

"Hey, kids," said Itani's stepmom. "Have some bannock and tea! I knew you'd all be coming at some point, so I made lots."

Itani grabbed a Frisbee-sized piece of bannock and began to break it up into smaller pieces for everyone. His stepmom brought the kettle and mugs over and poured them each a little bit of tea. When she wasn't looking, the kids snuck three or four heaping teaspoons of sugar into their tea and stirred. TJ wasn't usually allowed to put that much in, but he thought that he needed the extra energy because he had played out all morning and they were probably going to be playing out all afternoon too.

Once they finished eating, Itani asked

his stepmom, "Lisa, if my friends are allowed to sleep over, can you make *tuktu* stew?"

Lisa smiled. "Of course! We just got a big piece of tuktu from my ataata yesterday."

"Woohoo!" said Itani. He patted TJ on the back. Since TJ was already upset with Itani, he really didn't want to be touched.

But TJ tried to stay positive. He loved playing out, he loved camping and sleeping in tents, he loved tea and bannock, and he loved tuktu stew. That's a lot more good things than bad things.

CHAPTER 3
Getting Ready

After sitting and watching TV a bit to let their bannock digest, the kids got their outdoor clothes on again and made their way to each of their houses. They could have called their parents from Itani's, but the day was still beautiful, and it seemed more fun to march across town to ask about the sleepover.

The first stop was Sapa's house. Her parents said that it sounded like fun, but they were already planning to go to her grandparents' cabin for the night. Sapa was still allowed to play out for a couple more hours, but she'd need to be back home in time to eat and get ready to go.

The next stop was TJ's. His anaana said it was okay for him to sleep over. TJ was kind of hoping that she'd say no, but he didn't tell anyone that.

Next was Robert's house. He was also allowed to sleep over. TJ was relieved to know that he wouldn't be the only one sleeping over. His mood lightened up a little as they made their way to Martha's house, which was all the way at the end of town.

Martha's parents said she couldn't sleep over because she had to babysit that night. This dampened TJ's mood a little bit, because Martha was usually pretty good at calming Itani down when he got too excited about things. TJ tried not to think too much about it, though. He thought that Itani might be better behaved with his parents around.

After playing out some more, the kids started to feel tired and cold. They went their separate ways, but TJ and Robert said they'd go over to Itani's around six o'clock.

As they'd been playing out, Itani was still bothering TJ more than the others. When he got home, TJ wanted to talk to his anaana about how he was feeling. But every time he tried to say something, he felt like he was overreacting. TJ knew that Itani sometimes acted like that when he was excited, so maybe he would stop once he'd calmed down a bit.

In his room, TJ packed up his backpack for the night. He grabbed some extra-warm pyjamas and thick socks, some snacks, a flashlight, and a book about animals to read if he woke up before the others.

Just before six o'clock, Robert walked in to pick up TJ so they could go to Itani's together. TJ put on his backpack and grabbed his sleeping bag, which was too big for his backpack. Then they headed over to Itani's.

CHAPTER 4
Feeling Restless

When they got to Itani's, TJ and Robert could hear people behind the house, so they went around back. The tent was all set up and the voices were coming from inside. Robert and TJ opened the zipper and went inside to see Itani and his ataata.

"Hi!" Itani yelled in excitement.

"Hey, boys," said Itani's ataata. "You can leave your sleeping bags in here."

Inside the tent, there was a big piece of plywood to keep the ground even. At one end of the tent there were foam mattresses with lots of extra blankets and pillows on top. It was warm inside since Itani's ataata was using a camp stove for heating.

TJ and Robert put their sleeping bags down and joined Itani and his ataata on the mattresses.

Itani seemed even more excited than before, which TJ should have expected. Everything seemed kind of okay at first. They just played a couple of card games with Itani's ataata. TJ found that Itani wasn't singling him out anymore and hoped it would last all night.

"Hey, kids?" said a familiar voice from outside the tent. It sounded like Itani's stepmom.

Itani's ataata opened the zipper and checked. TJ saw him look around and then up at the house. "Hi!" he said.

"The food is ready!" called out Itani's stepmom.

"YES!" said Itani, yelling loudly right into TJ's ear. "I'm starving!"

TJ put a hand up to his ear, but it was already ringing. He didn't say anything, not wanting to be a party-pooper. They all went inside to eat. The food definitely made TJ feel a lot better. TJ, Robert, and Itani all had two or three bowls of tuktu stew and several pieces of bannock left over from lunch.

By the time they were all done eating, it felt like they couldn't move at all. They rested on the couch before going back outside to the tent. They watched some TV, but pretty soon Itani started getting restless. He jumped up from the couch and said, "Come on, let's go back to the tent!"

Robert got up without hesitation, so TJ got up too. Itani, in his impatience to get back outside, drummed his hands on TJ's shoulders as they walked to the porch to get their jackets on. TJ felt like he should say something now, before Itani started to act more wildly, but he didn't want to do it in front of Itani's parents.

"I'll be out soon to warm up the stove again, okay?" said Itani's ataata. The three boys headed outside.

"What do you want to do? Play hide-and-seek? Or cards? Or—" Itani said.

"Let's have a snowball fight!" said Robert.

Bad feelings rumbled inside TJ, but he thought that was an all-right idea since it was just the three of them. They each went to different areas that could work like shelters or forts, then they started to make snowballs. Robert slowly counted down. "Okay! Three…two…one…GO!"

It was fun at first. They were playing fair and not aiming for areas where getting hit would hurt. But once the game started to slow down a bit, Itani seemed to grow restless again. He ran out from behind his fort with an armful of snowballs. Since TJ's fort was closest to Itani's, he ran straight to TJ and threw a snowball from closer range. It hit TJ's chest, so when it burst, some snow went inside his jacket.

It really hurt, and the cold snow stung TJ's chest. It took a lot of effort for TJ not to cry. Itani just kept running, going off to hit Robert in the same way. TJ hoped that maybe Robert would say something to Itani about calming down, but Robert playfully yelled out, "Nooooo!"

After a few deep breaths, TJ calmed himself down. He decided he was going to tell Itani that it would be better if he started playing nicer, but just then Itani's ataata came out.

"Come on, boys! Let's warm up the tent and get ready to sleep," said Itani's ataata.

CHAPTER 5
Pillow Fight!

While Itani's ataata was warming up the camp stove, he told a story about a time he went out camping when he was their age. He had been at the camp with his parents and uncle when there was a polar bear swimming toward their cabin. They had to shoot their rifles into the air to scare the polar bear away.

As he'd been telling the story, the boys had all grown sleepy. Their eyes were heavy as they listened.

"All right, why don't you all go to sleep now," Itani's ataata said.

He turned the heat down on the camp

stove, made sure the kids were all bundled and warm, and then left the tent. Before zipping the tent back up, he said, "Be careful with the stove, okay, kids?"

As the boys settled in for the night, TJ found he was wide awake. With the cold air and absolute silence outside the tent, they all became a little bit hyper. Dread filled TJ as he realized what that might mean Itani would do.

"PILLOW FIGHT!" Itani called out as he smashed his pillow into TJ's head.

"Stop!" exclaimed TJ, shielding his head with his arms. But Itani laughed and kept hitting him with the pillow.

Robert quickly joined in, but TJ was upset. He'd had enough. All his feelings had built up. He got up and said, "I'm going home!"

Itani and Robert stopped playing.

Itani laughed, looking confused. "How come?" he asked.

"Because you've been bothering me all day!" TJ said. He gathered his things into his backpack and started to get his boots and jacket on.

"We were just playing, TJ," said Robert. "You should have told us you weren't having fun."

TJ didn't know what to say, so he didn't say anything. He unzipped the tent and stormed home.

CHAPTER 6
Talking Things Out

TJ didn't live far, but it was dark out. He ran all the way home, trying not to cry. When TJ walked inside, his anaana looked away from the TV, a mixture of confusion and worry on her face. She asked, "What's wrong, irniq?"

TJ still didn't know what to say, so he just started crying. Through his tears and short breaths, he stammered out, "Ita... Itani...Itani was bothering me all...all day and...and I just...I just wanted to come home."

TJ's anaana went over to comfort him. She wrapped her arms around TJ in a reassuring hug. "Aww, irniq. What was Itani doing to bother you?" she asked.

"He was just picking on me," TJ said, trying to calm down. "When we were playing games, he was being nice to everyone but me. He kept play-fighting me and touching me, and I wanted him to stop."

"Did you tell him that he was bothering you?" his anaana asked.

"Yeah," TJ said. "Kind of."

"Tell me about it," his anaana encouraged him.

TJ thought for a moment. He said, "I was going to try to tell him earlier, but I didn't want to do it in front of all our friends or his parents."

"I understand. You didn't want to embarrass him."

"Yeah, but I also didn't want anyone to think I was tattling on him," TJ said. "So then I just got really mad at him and left."

"Did you tell him why you were mad?" his anaana asked.

TJ shrugged. "Not really. I kind of felt weird about it."

"It sounds like Itani wasn't respecting your personal space," his anaana said.

TJ raised his eyebrows in agreement.

"I know it's hard to tell your friends when they're bothering you," said TJ's anaana. "But if something someone is doing is making you feel uncomfortable, then you have every right to speak up. I understand that maybe you didn't feel ready to talk to Itani about this, so I'm glad you talked to me." TJ's anaana hugged him tight. "Do you think you can talk to Itani about all this now that you've talked to me?" she asked.

"I think so," TJ said.

"Okay. Now why don't you go get some sleep? I'll call Itani's parents to tell them that you came home. Maybe tomorrow you can explain to Itani how you felt."

"Okay," said TJ, and he went off to bed.

The next day, after TJ had eaten breakfast and brushed his teeth, he got ready to head over to Itani's house. He was feeling bad for blowing up the way he did, and he knew what he was going to say. He hoped Itani would be willing to listen.

Robert had gone home, and Itani was in the tent starting to pack things up. TJ was able to squat down to see inside the tent through the open zipper. Itani saw TJ, but he kept packing his things.

"Hi," TJ said. Itani didn't seem happy, and he didn't say hi back. TJ continued, "I'm sorry that I got so mad yesterday. I should've told you how I was feeling before it got that bad."

"Yeah, you should've," said Itani.

"My anaana is always telling me to talk about my feelings more," TJ said. "I guess I'm still learning how to do that."

"What were you so mad about?" Itani asked.

"Well, sometimes you play a little rough." TJ continued, "I know we were playing tag, but I felt like you were in my personal space a lot. Just because you're my friend doesn't mean it's okay to touch me all the time. Even when you think it's no big deal."

Itani was quiet. Then he stopped rolling up his sleeping bag and looked over at TJ.

"I didn't realize that," Itani said. "I guess my brothers and sisters and I are always playing like that. I never thought that it might bug someone else. Sorry."

"Thanks," said TJ. "I still want to be friends. That's why I wanted to tell you all this."

"I still want to be friends too," Itani said, smiling. "I'll try not to play so rough from now on."

TJ smiled. Then he put his hand on Itani's arm and said, "TAG! YOU'RE IT!"

They spent the rest of the day much like the day before, running around and playing out with their friends. But this time, they were both much happier.

Inuktitut Glossary

Notes on Inuktitut pronunciation: There are some sounds in Inuktitut that may be unfamiliar to English speakers. The pronunciations below convey those sounds in the following ways:

- A double vowel (for example, *aa*, *ee*) creates a long vowel sound.
- Capitalized letters indicate the emphasis.
- q is a "uvular" sound, which is a sound that comes from the very back of the throat (the uvula). This is different from the k sound, which is the same as the typical English k sound.
- R is a rolled "r" sound.

For more Inuktitut and Inuinnaqtun pronunciation resources, please visit inhabiteducation.com/inuitnipingit.

anaana a-NAA-na	mother
anauligaaq a-now-li-GAAQ	Inuktitut baseball
ataata a-TAA-ta	father
irniq IR-niq	son
tuktu TOOK-tu	caribou

Nunavummi